Winter Cats

Janet Lawler

illustrated by Ela Smietanka

Albert Whitman & Company
Chicago, Illinois

To Josh, one cool cat!—JL

For my cat, Brush—ES

Library of Congress Cataloging-in-Publication data is on file with the publisher.

Text copyright © 2019 by Janet Lawler

Illustrations copyright © 2019 by Albert Whitman & Company

Illustrations by Ela Smietanka

First published in the United States of America in 2019 by Albert Whitman & Company

ISBN 978-0-8075-9124-6 (hardcover)

ISBN 978-0-8075-9125-3 (ebook)

Printed in China

10 9 8 7 6 5 4 3 2 1 HH 24 23 22 21 20 19

Design by Rick DeMonico

For more information about Albert Whitman & Company,
visit our website at www.albertwhitman.com.

100 Years of Albert Whitman & Company
Celebrate with us in 2019!

Willy was an indoor cat.
He'd never been outside.
"Our life inside is cozier,"
his mother said with pride.

"Those outdoor cats are weird and wild—they're not like us," said Dad.

But Willy wondered while he watched.
I bet they're not so bad.

One frosty dawn, he peeked outside…

and heard a joyful cry.
"On to Winter Carnival!"
cheered kitties sledding by.

So Willy crouched and tiptoed out
the open kitchen door.
He longed to join their festive games—
he had to see some more.

A tabby hailed him. "Hey, you're new!
Come try a downhill run."
Willy blinked. His whiskers twitched.
"Well—thanks! It looks like fun."

He swirled atop a sled of bark,
careening down the slope,
his tail entwined with one nearby
to make a steering rope.

Next they played on icicles
that hung along a roof.
A tiger cat said, "Please, you first!"

They landed with a poof!

Then all of them built snowball cats,
with acorns for the eyes,

before they flopped, creating shapes of angels just their size.

A calico held out her paw
and warned, "The pond is slick!"
Willy wobbled for a while
until he tried a trick.

He skated out and took a leap,
flying through the air.
The others clapped as Willy twirled
and landed with a flair.

Too soon the sun was setting.
Willy said, "I have to go!"
He added, "Come along with me.
I live indoors, you know."

They slipped inside and shook off snow.
Then Willy turned around.
He heard his mother scolding,
"What's this company you've found?"

The visitors cried, "Sorry, ma'am!"
and wiped the puddled floor.

Willy said, "These cats are nice.
We'd like to play some more."

And after all the games were done,
he said, "New friends, drink up!"
Milk dripped off their whiskers
while each guest enjoyed a cup.

Now indoor cats and outdoor cats
meet nearly every day,

together sharing friendship
during all the games they play.

Date: 10-25-19 **Initial:** DJ
Damage:
White stickers put on
inside front & Back covers
by staff.